#1 The Case of the Blowing Whistle

C.C. Beechum

Published by Ebenezer Publishing Co.
Worcester, MA
ISBN-13 9781469954486
ISBN-10 1469954486

Email the author at: ccbeechum@yahoo.com

To Tom and Andrew
My Beacons

Acknowledgements

Thank you to my family and friends and all who supported me in this project. A special thanks goes to my friend Liz for her ultimate support. Also, a special thanks goes to my mother for her guidance.

Chapter One
My Town

I live in a very small town called Acoomemeck (A coo mick). It was originally settled by Native Americans and named by them. Most towns around here were originally settled by Native Americans and named by them. They all sound like beautiful songs. Like most small towns everyone knows everyone in town and most of their business. Nobody knows the actual meaning of Acoomemeck, and it doesn't seem to bother anyone much that they don't. Every now and then someone will come to town and try to research the true meaning of the name. They spend numerous hours in the town library and interview all the oldest people in town. They go to surrounding towns and try to get information from there. They spend many hours researching and reading. They put a lot of effort into their research, and I think each person truly feels they will discover the true meaning of the name of our town. In spite of all their efforts they always come up with the same thing - nothing. There is no meaning to be found for the name of my town anywhere.

I think it's a cool name to have, so I've come up with a meaning for it. I thought about it for a long time, and I really considered the landscape here. I'd walk around my neighborhood and take notes about what I saw. I interviewed a few people like my mother and some neighbors. It took me a long time, but I finally came up with it, The Land of Beautiful Meadows, with a river running through it. I say it that way because that's the way the Native Americans would have said it.

Furthermore it sounds better that way. The reason I named it that is because there used to be a great number of meadows in my town according to my mother. There are pictures of the meadows in the town library and in my school. They look like beautiful places with tall grass and button shaped flowers growing wild. It must have been a great place to lay back and watch the clouds roll by.

The meadows have been replaced by stores, houses, and businesses. More Native Americans lived here back then, than the number of people living here now. Many Native Americans lived all over this part of the country, and there were quite a few of them living right in my town.

I guess I know just about everyone in town, and they know me. There isn't much excitement here, and sometimes it can get boring. My mother keeps saying that someday she'd like to move away, but we never do. I like my town even though it's very small. We need all the stores and houses we have, but I wish we had some of those meadows back. They would be a great place to have ball games, picnics, and play hide and go seek in.

My parents grew up in this town with their parents, my grandparents. My family has lived here a long time. The town was settled in the seventeen hundreds, 1715 to be exact, and it hasn't grown all that much over the years. I guess that's what happens to some places they just get forgotten. They just stay small and never really grow.

Chapter Two
North Street Elementary School

My school was built in 1896. You might not think that was a long time ago, but Paul Revere's great grand children could have come here. Well, they didn't actually come here, but they could have?

The outside of my school is brick. Not the bright clean, red brick you see nowadays, but that old red brick with white spots on it where it has been patched up to keep it from falling down. Every three feet or so there's a huge white spot, which I'm told is cement (mortar), covering up some crumbling old brick. There are holes and spider webs with spiders and dead flies in them. There is a lot of mortar in those holes, and it makes the school look ugly - really ugly!

The windows are practically falling out of their frames from age. The glass has a cloudy look to it, and it's even broken in some spots way up high at the steeple. There are 15 windows on the front of the school and fifteen on the back. They are large windows with ugly green frames. All of them have shades except for the ones way at the top. A few of them have things on them like snowflakes or butterflies, and some even have paper flowers hanging from them.

My classroom has large stars hanging from the shades. My teacher made them a long time ago and hung them up. They are all different colors and have different color sparkles on them. They are very light and airy, and they twirl in the wind when it blows. They are something to look at if it gets boring, but it hardly ever does.

It's not a really big school. Actually it's the smallest in town. Most people like it the best because anyone who was important went here. An addition was added on to it a few years back because it was way too small. While the addition took place my mom said they held school in the town hall. They used the offices there, and even the town hall was too small.

I mean all the mayors and police officers since 1896, and most of the older teachers went here. There are many pictures of my school in the town library, and you can see the changes it has undergone over the years. It started out as a one-room schoolhouse because the town was really small back then. The one-roomed schoolhouse was torn down ages ago and replaced with the building that's there now, plus the addition.

There are only two elementary schools in town, so the fact that most people went here is not really all that surprising. The other school in town was built in the eighties, 1982 to be exact, and it's on the other side of town.

Not very many people live on the other side of town now or even go to that school for that matter. There used to be a big mill over there, and it employed almost everyone in town. It closed down a few years ago because it didn't get enough business to stay open. The mill was the only place in town where you could work for a long time. People thought the mill would stay open forever.

The building is still there, and I sometimes go over there to visit my friend Megan White. Megan goes to school there, and she likes it very much. The name of that school is Potter Hill Elementary School. We walk to the mill sometimes and check out what is left. It's kind of sad to see a huge building so quiet with no one in it. Megan says it's haunted, and we never go inside. Someday I'd like to go in and explore it. Maybe I can convince Megan the next time I go visit her.

Slowly other stuff came to town like big banks, grocery stores, and doctors' offices. Now we even have a McDonald's. Well, it's about five miles from my house and we never go, but it's there nonetheless.

Most people worked at the mill or someone in their family did, or they knew someone who did. My mom worked there when she was a young girl. Now she works at the hospital in town as a nurse. The name of the hospital is St. Ignatius. That is such a weird name you almost think it's made up. I looked it up on the Internet, and there it was, St. Ignatius. He was born in Spain and lived really close to the King and Queen of Spain.

My mom works long hours at the hospital, and she is tired a lot. I think it's because it's the only hospital in town. My mom is not too young and not too old. She has short brown hair and long eyelashes with blue eyes. She is five feet six inches tall and is medium build. She was skinny when she was young just like me. People tell me I look just like her. I can't see it yet, but maybe someday I will.

I'm home by myself after school most days, but I don't really mind. I read a lot and do all my homework and talk on the phone, well sometimes I talk on the phone. I don't have many close friends, but that is one of my goals for this year. You have to set goals for yourself otherwise what is there to look forward to?

My mom is usually home for supper right around 5 o'clock, and if she isn't Mrs. Munson from next-door calls and invites me there for supper. Mrs. Munson is our next-door neighbor on the right and Ben Walters is our neighbor on the left. He is my best male friend. He doesn't like to admit that we're friends, but we are, and we hang out together often.

Mrs. Munson is older than my mom. The reason I know this is because she has white hair, and she is retired. She is not very tall and kind of round. Mrs. Munson doesn't have any children, and she was never married. She used to teach Language at my school, but she retired about ten years ago and travels to many interesting places and volunteers at the hospital.

She's very helpful and cooks all kinds of great stuff for us. Her house smells like peppermint though, and I love to hear the phone ring and hear her say, “okay, she’ll be right home.” She always gives me a plate for my mom on these days and two desserts. I guess my mom and she are great friends.

A few years ago a lot of people had babies, and they grew up, so that is why they built a new school on the other side of town. The population of our town is very low, 5,785 with an elevation of 1,304 miles. I only know this because it says it on a sign as you leave town, and every time we drive out of town to go to the mall my mom points it out. I mean I get it! But, she still says it every time.

The steeple of my school is made out of iron. It’s long and skinny and shaped like an ice cream cone, an upside down one. I guess it’s some sort of lightning rod or other. I’ve never seen it struck by lightning, which I’m sure is a very good thing. A few years ago it did get struck by lightning, and everyone was afraid that the school would burn down. I thought that was the purpose of a lightning rod to prevent fires? Oh well.

Under the steeple is a sort of lookout area. It's a small room with four tiny windows, one is cracked, and it looks like a spider web. The windows don't have any shades on them, and they are dirty.
The outside of the room has the look of a jigsaw puzzle that doesn't have any connecting pieces. I guess you could say like a gingerbread house. That is of course if you believe in that stuff.

I'm not sure what that room could have possibly been used for because it's way too small for a classroom and way too high up for any normal person to use, but I'd really like to find out. I guess I'm just a curious kind of person, and I like to know about things. I look up there all the time on my way home from school and try to figure out what in the world that room was used for?

I'm sure everyone inside the school knows how ridiculous this all looks to a newcomer, but no one seems to care. They just march right up onto the stoop, ring the bell and go on in. We don't often have newcomers to our school, but when we do I wished the school looked better.

The stoop has a date cemented right into it. The date is made out of pieces of blue marble and a milky colored glass. The number one has a big hole in it, and half of the top of the one is chipped off and worn away and dirty. The outline of the numbers is so faint you have to rely on the marble to tell what year it is. It looks very lame even though it has a fancy design around it, and it ends up to be a big bow all tied up. It looks like it took a really long time to make. It's one of the nicest things about my school besides the lookout. The date is 1896.

My name is Penelope Barrows. I'm eleven years old, and I'm in fifth grade. I have very long brown and blonde hair. I like to wear it down on most days. Occasionally I wear clips in it or in a ponytail. I'm kind of tall but not too tall, and I'm very skinny. I'm an only child, so I don't have a little brother in second grade like almost everyone else in town. I do get a lot more Christmas presents than anyone I know, which in itself is fine, but I really wish I had a little brother to play with sometimes.

My grandmother was named Penelope, and there it is. Her great, great grandmother was named Penelope, and she came over on some boat with a ton of other people and decided to live here. I guess it was a long trip, and some people died, but I'm told fifth grade is the place to find out about it. My mom told me the whole story when I was eight, but I forgot most of it because she always cries when she tells it, and I end up concentrating on her and not on the story. I'm not sure why she cries, but I guess it's what some adults do when they tell stories.

My dad died when I was born. He was in the Gulf War, and he just didn't come home. He was tall with brown and blonde hair, and he had very blue eyes. He had a great smile, and when I look at pictures of him his smile always makes me smile right back at him. My mom was real sad for a long time she told me, but I never met him, so I'm sad too, but he looks real handsome in his uniform in the picture above the fireplace on the mantle. I use that picture in my mind whenever someone talks about their father.

My mother and I live alone about five blocks from my school. Our house is gray with green shutters. It is kind of a big house for two people, but I guess my mom and dad had planned on more than just one child. We have a big yard with some trees in it. My mom loves to plant flowers, so we have all different kinds of flowers growing in flowerbeds all over the yard. My grandma used to live with us, and she would tell me stories about my mom and dad, but she died last year right around Christmas time. She was very sick with cancer, and I was very sad, mostly for my mother. I guess many people have died in my life, but It's okay. It makes me feel sad sometimes, and I miss them, but my mom talks about them so much I feel very close to them.

When I miss my grandma sometimes Mrs. Munson tells me stories about her, and she makes me feel warm inside again, and I don't miss her so much. Mrs. Munson and my grandma were great friends, and she misses her too. Grandpa died way before I was born, so I never knew him. It is very odd Mrs. Munson's stories always have grandpa in them, so I feel I know him just the same. One story was about how grandpa proposed to grandma. He took her out to dinner and put her engagement ring in her glass of champagne. I think it's a really silly thing to do. What if she drank it? Nonetheless, I enjoy the stories.

My mom drives me to school most days, but occasionally she let's me walk with Ben Walters our next-door neighbor. He's in sixth grade, and so he's cool. He thinks so anyway.

He's tall and skinny with bony knees. He has kind of long brown hair, and I think he should get it cut. Ben LOVES baseball and talks about it constantly. He has two younger brothers, and he lives with them and his mom and dad. He grew up in Acoomemeck and wants to leave when he gets older.

Last year he went to the Baseball Hall of Fame in Cooperstown, NY. His family asked my mother if I could go with them, but the thought of all those hours in the family van with three boys did not sound like fun to me, so I said no.

I think he kind of likes me because he's always hitting me on the arm and running, so I can catch up with him and hit him back. At least that's what Mrs. Neederman says.

I know, I know her name is crazy, but she is okay. Mrs. Neederman is my teacher. She wears black to school almost everyday with a ton of silver jewelry and mostly platform heels. Her hair is wild and curly, but occasionally she straightens it, and it looks really slick. Sometimes she wears another color, and everyone just about goes crazy. Not me though, I love black, and when I grow up I want to dress just like her.

Ben says she's a weirdo, but that's what most boys say about their teachers. Boys don't really know too much, but they're fun to have around when you're playing baseball or soccer or hide and go seek.

Penelope is a very uncommon name, and every teacher that hears it says, "ahhhh that's a sweet name. Was it your grandmothers?"

I get called Nellie a lot, which I don't really mind, well most of the time anyway. But, it does kind of sound like a boy.

Fifth grade is like fifteen minutes before the Jello is ready, being cool but not quite done. Most people say I act grown up for my age. I think it's because I'm an only child. That's what my mom tells me. The fact is that most of the sixth graders are not jelled at all, but they are in sixth grade and the oldest in the school, not including the teachers of course.

There are 31 sixth graders this year. It is such a big class that they eat lunch alone in their classroom because we can't all fit in the lunchroom at the same time. It is such a tiny lunchroom that our school has three separate lunches. Maybe they will build another addition to our school? You never know? I had to go in the sixth grade classroom one time last week to pass around some paper for teachers to sign, and I didn't like it very much. The room smelled like pickles and sour milk. I wondered how they could do their math after lunch with such a bad smelling room.

When they built my school it was right in the middle of a big meadow. It was called Potter's Meadow. The meadow had so many colorful wildflowers growing in it with big dots right in the middle of them. The kids in town used to play games in the field and run all through it everyday. That must have been some fun. There aren't too many meadows anymore in town.

Now there are a lot of buildings and stuff, and people are always complaining that there needs to be more space. Some of the wildflowers still grow in the back of the school. I pick them after school sometimes and bring them to my mom. She loves those flowers and so do I. I often wonder why this school is called North Street Elementary, and the school across town is called Potter's Elementary. I mean this school was built on Potter's Field but not named after it?

There were houses back then of course, but they weren't all close by and crowded together. They were built closer to the river that flows through the town. It's called the Greenstone River, and the Native Americans named that too. The houses in the olden days were about 2 miles away from the school, and the kids would walk to school everyday! Boy that must have been great.

Chapter Three
A History Lesson

1896,1897,1898, and so on and so on - there are tons of them. A couple of years are missing, but all the class pictures are in a big glass case with metal trimming around it. People call it a bunch of memorabilia stuff or something like that. This large glass case is right in the middle of the first floor of my school. There are many trophies and plaques and emblems with different years on them. The dates on some of them are worn off like someone had it outside the case and then put it back in there? The trophies are mainly for sports, and it seems that at one time there was a fairly good basketball team that played for this school.

There is even a class picture with my mother in it. Mom kind of looks like me, but not really. It's cool to see your mom when she was young. Some of the other kids in my town are embarrassed by the pictures, but not me, I enjoy them all. The one of Mrs. Munson and my grandmother is hysterical and makes me laugh out loud. I think someone should dust all the stuff off in there. It looks all filmy like no one cares about it. I care about it, and maybe I should ask the principal if I could clean it up sometime.

Now I guess I wouldn't mind walking to school everyday because I only live five blocks away, but two miles? I think that would be hard even for me, and I play soccer and softball at recess and everything. I guess kids back then liked to walk or something. They walked home for lunch too. Believe it or not their mom's were waiting for them with lunch and big smiles. Mrs. Munson says she loved to eat lunch at home with her mom and baby brother, but I can't understand it.

Wow! That must have been so boring eating lunch alone without your friends to talk to. I guess that's why kids looked so weird back then. I mean eight miles a day and all?

There are pictures in the hallway of some of these kids and the meadow and the houses. The pictures look so old, and the kids are dressed so funny. I guess that's how they dressed back then. As the years go on the pictures look better to me. Somehow I like the oldest ones best. The kids look like they need a friend and sometimes, so do I. I think one of them is the mayor of my town. He was 6 in the picture. That doesn't seem really strange to me, and I don't know why everyone thinks it's such a big deal. I mean everyone goes to school. Right?

On this day in school we are learning how to write a letter. I think it's dumb to learn how to write a letter with the Internet and all, but Mrs. Neederman says it's very important to learn, and anyway Mrs. Munson will help me. I know she will because she has hundreds of letters under her bed in a shoebox, and if anyone knows how to write letters it's Mrs. Munson all right. I guess she wrote to everyone she knew because that box sure is full.

Michael Anderson keeps talking out, and Mrs. Neederman looks upset.

Finally she calls his name and says, "Michael will you please pay attention."

Michael responds with a, "Yes Mrs. Neederman."

Everyone else giggles because she always says that, and he always says that, but he never stops talking. Michael is very tall for his age and skinny. He has red hair and a ton of freckles. He never stops talking and interrupts people when they are talking. He can be very annoying. I think Michael has a sad life, but I can't prove it.

Sarah Hanson raises her hand and asks, " Can we write in pen Mrs. Neederman?"

Mrs. Neederman says as she shuts the classroom door, " I think we should wait until our final draft to use our pens Sarah, don't you?" Everyone nods and agrees with the teacher and goes back to work.

Sarah said with her head over her letter and her pencil erasing, "Mrs. Neederman I think that's a very good idea. I've already made a few changes, and pen would be messy."

Sarah is very short with long, thick, black hair. She is probably the smartest girl in the class. She is an only child like me, so we have a lot in common. When I don't know something I ask Sarah. She is in my reading group, and we work together all the time. I would like to be better friends with her. I will put her down as one of my goals.

The letter I'm writing is to my mom. I'm going to ask her how she likes her job. I guess I already know how she likes her job, but I have to pick someone to write to. I write the date in the upper right corner. I put the greeting down with a comma and write my mother's name. Andrea Barrows. I start to write my letter. Dear Andrea, What do you do at St. Ignatius Hospital? I like my first sentence and continue to work on my letter. I hope to finish this in school, so I won't have any homework.

At lunch I asked Michael why he kept asking all those silly questions?

He just said, "Shut-up weirdo, it's none of your business."

So, I sat down to eat my lunch with Stephanie, Michael, and Peter.

At recess I asked Michael again why he always talks out.

Michael answered me as he was running up the stairs out the door, " I don't know why but, it's hard not to. Maybe I'm a talking machine."

Michael says some fairly dumb things sometimes.

Stephanie and I are best friends. She has short blonde hair and green eyes. She's average height and always wears a sweatshirt even when it's warm. She has two moms, one dad and a baby brother. I'm not positive what it means to have two moms, but she sure is nice, and she is always fair. I asked my mom what it means to have two mothers, and she said she'd tell me when I get older. She says that when she doesn't want to tell me something, so it must be a long story.

Today I have a bagel and cream cheese, an apple, some carrots and milk. How I wish my mom wasn't so healthy. Being a nurse and all she makes me eat all this healthy stuff all the time. On the days she's late, and I go over Mrs. Munson's, I get to take her desserts to school. Yummy! I always split them with Stephanie, so she gives me some of her snack sometimes too.

During Social Studies the principal Mrs. Villanus comes over the loud speaker and announces that the North Street School tee shirts have arrived. My mother bought me one, and I couldn't wait to get it. It is blue with our school mascot on it. This year our school mascot was a shark. The shark has big fangs on it. Molly Cooper in grade five drew the mascot. You see we had a contest in October of last year, and she won. She's in grade six now, and boy is she proud!

I kept thinking about the tee shirts all afternoon until finally the box arrived. The custodian Mr. Murphy brought the box up to us and plopped it on the floor with a big thud. There were beads of sweat on his forehead, and it looked like he might pass out at any minute. He asked Mrs. Neederman to count them, and he rested his arm on the doorjamb to wipe his forehead with his other arm's sleeve.

As he was leaving he said, "Let me know if you need anymore tee shirts. There are more in the office, and we have some left over sweatshirts too."

Mrs. Neederman thanked him and he left.

He didn't pass out of course, and he went to the next room with their box. Everyone got a tee shirt except Michael. Michael hardly ever got anything. Like we order books sometimes and Michael never gets any. That's one of the reasons why I think Michael is sad. Maybe I'll put him on my list of goals too.

We were all excited, and Mrs. Neederman gave up asking us to be quiet. We tried the tee shirts on and laughed at how big some of them were. Stephanie's was so big that I think it may have been for her father or something. Mine fit fairly well, and I kept it on over my other shirt. In line at the end of the day it was funny to see a sea of blue tee shirts walking down the street. It made me giggle and smile.

On my way home that day I made sure to look up at that lookout. I did this everyday thinking I could figure out what it was used for. I had asked my mom so many times what she thought it was used for that I knew better not to ask her anymore. She just didn't know. As a matter of fact no one in town knew. Well, the people in town that I knew anyway.

After supper Stephanie called me, and we met out in front of my house. She lived about seven houses down the street, and I saw her mother wave to me as Stephanie entered our driveway. Stephanie's mother was very pretty and was always dressed up in fine clothes. She worked in Boston and made a lot of money. Stephanie always had new clothes and fancy shoes.

We played hopscotch and talked and hung out for a while. We talked about Michael for a bit, and we decided to be nicer to him even though he was annoying most times. We agreed he seemed sad and thought maybe he needed a friend. This was a tough goal, but I thought maybe it was a noble one.

Steph's mother called around seven, and said it was time for Stephanie to go home. Stephanie was a good friend. She was my only friend really besides Ben and Megan, so I missed her when she couldn't come over. We did many things together, but she babysat for her brother sometimes, and that kept her busy too.

The next day in school was very much the same as the last, but it was different in the fact that it was Friday. We had Music, Art, and Gym on Friday. Fridays are my favorite day.

Mr. Horan the gym teacher did all kinds of exciting games with the class. Today was the championship finals for beanbag throwing. You had to throw a beanbag through a large wooden face with the eyes, nose, and mouth cut out. You had three beanbags, and each hole had a different point value. Stephanie and I were on different teams. She had Michael and Ben on her team. I had Emma and Josh on mine. It was a very close final game, but my team did not win. Stephanie's team did not win. The team that won was extremely excited and started yelling really loudly. They yelled so loudly that the principal came in and asked if everything was all right.

Friday meant that Stephanie would sleep over, and we could paint our toenails and eat chips and drink soda. We looked forward to it every week- well almost every week. We did this as much as we could. My mom was cool sometimes, especially on sleepovers.

All day in school I kept tapping my feet and twisting my hair. These were nervous habits that I couldn't really control because I wanted the weekend to come so badly. Finally the bell rang, and I practically ran down Harry Strand from the fourth grade running out of the door.

I could hear Mrs. Needernman's voice in the distance saying, "Slow down Penelope the building is not on fire."

Why do teachers say such strange things?

In my mother's car I turned the music down low, so I could talk to her about the weekend festivities. Then I saw her face as she was changing the radio station, "Penelope I have some bad news. Stephanie cannot come over this weekend."

I thought I heard her wrong and kept right on talking.

"Penelope are you listening?"

I wasn't.

"Penelope!"

I was listening, my mother hardly ever yelled.

"What?" I said, not wanting to hear the news.

As my mom was turning the car into the driveway she said, " I'm sorry honey Stephanie cannot come over this weekend. I have to work at the hospital all weekend. A number of nurses are out with some stomach virus, and I have to fill in."

Is this a glimmer of hope? I can go over there?

Then she said locking the doors to the car, "Stephanie's mom is very sick and needs Stephanie to take care of her baby brother Derek. Derek is three and needs her attention."

"ARRRGGHHHHH! Why me I yelled!" as I was getting out of the car.

"Now, now Penelope, Mrs. Munson has agreed to spend the whole weekend with you," she said walking to the front door. "She even said she'd take you to the new museum outside of town and to the park and"...

I wasn't listening, Mrs. Munson? Are you kidding me! Mrs. Munson? ARRRGGGHHHH!

Chapter Four
Mrs. Munson

My face must have told the story because Mrs. Munson was so nice to me I thought I was going to throw up.

"Nellie would you like a second helping of dessert?" she said to me as she was carrying over pecan pie to the table.

Knowing dessert was the one thing I would love a second helping of but was too shy to ask.... I didn't take the second helping, but just sat there and brooded.

"No thank you Mrs. Munson I'm full," I wasn't.

As Mrs. Munson was clearing the dinner dishes she said, "What shall we do now that dinner is over? Would you like to go to the park?" It was late in May and still light out, so I said we should go for a walk.

"Sure Mrs. Munson I'd love to" I said, as I was putting on my sweater.

Stephanie's house was down the street, and I was hoping Stephanie would be outside with her baby brother or something. Often times Stephanie would be outside minding her brother in the yard. He was little and needed to be watched closely.

Walking down the street I looked up at the lookout as I always do. I half expected the lookout to be full of people just to fool me. It was shining in the sun and empty. The sun was hitting the windows just right and making them difficult to see. I put my hand over my eyes to see. I was staring upward and thinking about the weekend when I thought I noticed something flash up there.

As I got closer and closer my stomach was starting to turn over and over with excitement. What if there was something up there, and I, Penelope Barrows had discovered it? My picture and a plaque would go into the glass case at school. I would be famous! People would walk up to me and ask me for my autograph. I wouldn't even charge them a dime. When the school was right in front of me I realized that I hadn't seen anything, and I figured it was just a reflection or the sun glimmering off the windowpane or something. Stephanie's yard was empty, and her house looked like no one was in it? Hmmpphh! Nobody. Nothing! Blah! I wonder where everyone could be?

I can honestly say as the night wore on Mrs. Munson was looking better and better to me, so I asked her some questions about North Street Elementary School.

"Mrs. Munson" I said, as I was eating some yummy potato chips, "What teacher did you like the best when you were in the fifth grade?"

"Well, I believe I liked Mrs. Carrol the best. She loved to sing and was always merry. We sang songs every chance we could" she said, as she was popping a chip into her mouth.

"What subject did you like the best?" I then asked her.

As Mrs. Munson was changing the channel on the television she said, " Oh, I believe I liked History the best. It can be so fascinating! What's your favorite subject Nellie?"

I'm not really sure why talking about school was so interesting to me, but Mrs. Munson sure did know quite a lot about it. As I relaxed from the disappointment of the day her stories became quite interesting, and we talked for a long while.

I was only half listening when the phone rang. It was my mom checking up on us.

"Penelope I am going to be home very late, and I have to leave very early in the morning. Do you mind sleeping at Mrs. Munson's tonight? My mom said, as I was crunching on a chip.

"Well, I have never stayed at Mrs. Munson's Mom, and I wonder can you die from the smell of peppermint?"

My mother didn't think this was humorous, but she laughed anyway. I gave the phone to Mrs. Munson as she walked into the room.

"Of course, no problem, sure, okay, take care" a few times and I knew I was staying. Ughhh! How boring is this!

No Stephanie, no Mom, just Mrs. Munson! We ate chips and drank Coke. We watched some movie on television until ten o'clock or so. I'm not sure what it was about really, but there was some kissing and hugging and love stuff. At least she ate junk food and drank Coke. She said we needed to rest because we were going to have such a busy day tomorrow. I doubted she could ever tire me out, but I humored her and went to bed. As I was changing into my Hello Kitty pajamas I heard a whistle blowing off in the distance and wondered who would be blowing a whistle so late at night? And for what? I heard it two more times. That was three times in all. My eyes closed, and I went off to dreamland.

When I woke up in the morning it was raining. It was raining so hard that the window was difficult to see through. When it started to thunder I found myself running for cover under my blankets on my bed. Mrs. Munson was still sleeping, so I went into the kitchen and poured myself some orange juice. The orange juice tasted so good that I had another glass. By the time Mrs. Munson came down it was 8 o'clock, and I was starving. She made blueberry pancakes with real blueberries that she had picked last summer and home fries seasoned with spices that Mom really should get -bacon cooked just right and blueberry syrup. It tasted so good I had seconds.

As I was wolfing down the food I wondered why Mrs. Munson had never gotten married. I mean the pictures of her when she was young were well, cute. She looked so nice all dressed up on Sunday when she went to church, and it just seemed a bit strange to me. My mom had said that she was engaged once, but it didn’t work out. I wonder what had happened that made her change her mind.

The rain continued all morning, but it didn’t hold Mrs. Munson back.

She yelled up to me, “Hurry up we have to get going, get dressed.”

I shouted back from the top of the stairs, "Going in the shower now. I'll be down in ten."

I took a shower and got dressed quickly. I wore my new jeans and a white top with cut outs on it and sparkly things. My aunt Susan gave it to me for my birthday in October. My aunt Susan lives in Chicago with her family. She is my mother's only sibling, and they are very close. I thought the shirt was odd at the time because it had short sleeves, and October can get cold, but I was thankful for it now. It was perfect to go visit a museum in. On the way to the museum I wondered if the museum was going to be boring. I had gone to similar places on field trips, but field trips were hardly ever boring because we got to be away from school and all.

Chapter Five
The Museum

When we walked into the museum the woman at the desk knew Mrs. Munson and waved to her.

She smiled a lot at me and said, “What’s your name?”
I answered, “Penelope Barrows” politely and continued on.

They talked a minute about the weather, and then we went in.

I had never been to this museum; I mean it's new and all. The paintings in it were very cool. There were hundreds of them, and we stopped and looked at each one.

Mrs. Munson stared at a few for a long time, and as she was doing this she said to me, “Take your time Penelope enjoy the paintings. They are so beautiful. I enjoy each one.”

Well, I didn’t let on that they were very interesting to me also, but I did enjoy that place.

I just answered her as we turned the corner, “ I do believe that some of these paintings are in a book at school Mrs. Munson. I have seen that one before.”

I pointed to my left. It was a painting by John Singer Sargent, some famous guy.

Some of the paintings were by famous artists, but I didn’t recognize most of the names. Monday in school I’m going to ask Mrs. Neederman if she ever heard of them? Maybe even look some of them up on the Internet.

At lunch in the museum cafe Mrs. Munson said I could order anything I wanted.

So when the waitress came over and asked me what I wanted I said, “Macaroni and cheese please and a large Coke,” something my mom would never have let me have.

Mrs. Munson ordered a grilled cheese and a coffee. Everything was delicious, and the day wasn’t as bad as I thought it was going to be.

For dessert we had chocolate souffle, something I had never heard of. It was really chocolaty, and it had vanilla ice cream and hot fudge served with it. I was very full after lunch and was looking forward to walking around again.

After lunch we went to the Modern Wing. It was full of pictures of things I had never seen before? I mean people were oohing and awwing over them like, like... they were pictures of people or something. I liked that floor, but I didn't really understand it very well.

The next wing was Egyptian Art. Boy those Egyptians sure did do a lot of sculpting and painting. They used symbols to write called hieroglyphics and regular people couldn't understand them, only Egyptians.

As we were walking down a narrow corridor Mrs. Munson said, "Penelope the Egyptians used a tool to take out the parts of the body that could not be mummified. Then they put them in jars called canopic jars. The Egyptians believed in an "afterlife," which means a life after death. They buried themselves with all these things you see here."

I really didn't say too much as I was fascinated by all the things that they were buried with. It seemed to me that they were buried with all the things that they had when they were alive. There were combs and hair jewelry, clothes made out of all beads and cups and plates and even cats. Mrs. Munson told me a lot about the Egyptians, and I must say it was extremely interesting.

The last wing we went to was dedicated to local artists. As I went through the hall I didn't recognize one name. I mean I've lived in this town my whole life. You would think I would know someone? Nope, not a one! Mahoney, Banks, Melrose, Robinson, Highland, nope!

When I came to the second to the last painting I stopped for a long time. It was a painting of a family. In the painting it was bright and sunny out, but the faces on the people looked so gloomy. It was a mom, a tall girl, and two little boys who looked to be around two. The girl looked to be five or so. She was tall for her age at least she looked that way to me. I mean I don't remember coming to my mom's shoulders at age five. The reason I thought she was five was because she had a lunchbox in her hand with Princess Jasmine on it. No one would have a Princess Jasmine lunchbox unless they were in Kindergarten, so that makes her five.

The picture was painted seven years ago. Seven years ago!! That's like when I was four going on five. I wondered who those people were. I had never seen them in school or in town or even noticed anybody that looked like the mother or the daughter anywhere. Where were they? The daughter would be just about my age, and I definitely would have noticed her. The eyes were very blue. It was signed M. Robinson.

On the way home from the museum I began thinking about the family in the painting when my stomach started to ache, too much ice cream and junk food. I wondered if they lived on the other side of town, and that's why I didn't know them. I put my hand over my stomach and groaned.

I swear I had gained ten pounds in two days. No problem though. I was too skinny for my age, so the pediatrician told my mom, so I was really doing something good for myself. I just hoped my teeth wouldn't rot out before my mom came home.

Chapter Six
Ben and Flowers

When we got home the rain had stopped, and Ben was outside with his brothers playing tag on the front lawn. They were running and screaming and pulling each other onto the wet lawn. Ben's mom had come out twice while I was getting out of the car and going into the house, and I could see that she was not smiling.

"Mrs. Munson can I go out and play tag with Ben?" I said.

She just said, "May I" and nodded and smiled.

I took that as a yes and ran from the house. I mean Ben can be okay for a boy, and like I said before he is good at tag and some sports.

Ben pretended I was intruding, but I knew better. He was dying to get away from his brothers. They could be so childish sometimes.

As I walked over to him he said, "Hey Nellie, what ya doing? Want to play tag?"

I pretended not to hear him, and said," Let's go play tag in the school recess yard."

He thought about it for a moment and then said, "Okay race you," and off we went.

First of all, I didn't want to hang out with his little brothers, and second of all I wanted to pick some flowers for Mrs. Munson.

You see I view Mrs. Munson in a whole new way now. I actually liked spending time with her. She's very smart even for a teacher, and she really cares about what happens to my mom and me. So...flowers would be great to give to her at the very least.

When we got to the schoolyard there were a few teenagers hanging out at the basketball hoop smoking cigarettes. The first boy was tall and lanky with dark hair. He was dressed in black jeans, a white tee shirt and red sneakers. Red sneakers? Really! The other two boys looked like brothers. One was very tall and broad. The other one was slight of build with big muscles. They both had regular blue jeans on and black tee shirts. One had cowboy boots on, and the other one had on work boots. I guess they went to the high school, but I didn't ask.

There was one girl with them, and she looked to be the oldest of all. She was very pretty with medium length blonde hair. She had small features and was
slim. She wasn't smoking, but she did look kind of serious about the

conversation she was having with the three boys.

I heard her say, “No, no we can’t.”

She had on a cool pair of skinny jeans and a vest over her shirt. She looked upset and turned her back to us when we walked by them. When the boys saw us they left with the girl. I don’t know why they left. They probably didn’t want to be seen with little kids.

Ben and I went around back, and I picked some flowers for Mrs. Munson. The flowers felt stiff in my hand, and they didn’t really smell all that much. They were Coreopsis. I know this because I had picked these very same flowers for my mom, and we looked it up together on the Internet. I just love to Google things!

We didn’t feel like playing tag, so we sat on the hill behind the school and lay back on the grass and looked up at the clouds. We put blades of grass in our mouths and chewed on them.

Ben asked me, “What do you see up in the clouds Nellie?” as he was chewing on a blade of grass.

I answered him hesitantly, “Well, I don’t see anything right now, but when I do I will let you know.”

We saw all kinds of things in the clouds, and we lay there for what seemed like an hour.

After a long time I said to Ben,” I see an Egyptian, which I’m sure is directly related to my visit to the museum, a cat and a bus.”

Ben said, “I see some weird army guy with a machete and a rabbit.”

We both laughed long and hard. The clouds rolled on forever. It was sunny and warm. It was the first pleasant day of spring.

I was staring up at the little room I called the lookout daydreaming about going to Egypt when I saw it! I thought I was imagining things, but no I saw it! I mean her! She was up in that little room looking down on us. She wasn't standing exactly. She was peering over the windowsill ever so slightly, but I saw her. I couldn't exactly make out what she looked like, but I saw a girl! It was a girl with long brown hair. Well, at least it wasn't to her shoulders that I know for sure.

"Hey, look, look!!" I shouted to Ben.

"What?" he absently replied.

He had missed her and didn't seem all that interested. Maybe just maybe, I hadn't seen anything at all.

All sorts of thoughts raced through my head. I thought maybe it was the teenagers from the front schoolyard. So, I jumped up and raced to the front of the school. I ran halfway down the street until I realized that they had gone the other way. I stared over in the direction that they had walked and saw little bitty people walking towards the town hall. It wasn't them up there.

I raced back to the hill to see Ben still lying there with the piece of grass in his mouth and a grin on his face.

"What's the hurry Nellie?" he jeered.

"It's Penelope to you" I said and, "I saw..I saw..a girl..!"

"What? Where?" says Ben, as he rises and looks up to where I am pointing!

"Up there! Up there! In the lookout, look!"

As we both looked up to the sky towards the lookout both of us saw nothing. Nothing! I started to walk away with my head hanging down.

"Wait up Penelope, wait up!" Ben shouted.

On the way home Ben was silent and so was I. I know I saw her! What should I do? Nothing?

When we got closer to home Ben said to me, "You're crazy Nellie.

You have to forget about it. It was the sun in your eyes or something."

He teased me all the way up the walkway and said, "You're seeing things Nellie it can't be true," and laughed and giggled at me needing glasses.

I didn't appreciate him teasing me. I went through the door to Mrs. Munson's house, plopped down in her big easy chair and said, "See you tomorrow Ben," out the side window.

I told Mrs. Munson and she said, "It was probably just a reflection of the trees. Nellie why don't you go lie down before dinner."

That night when my mom came home I told her, she said, "Penelope, I think maybe you're over tired from your visit with Mrs. Munson. Why don't you have some dinner and go to bed early."

So that's just what I did. But, I wasn't overtired.

None of these things were true. I saw her, and she knew it, and so did I.

Chapter Seven
School

School UGGHH!

On Monday in school I said, "Mrs. Neederman have you ever heard of a painter called Degas (DEE-Gas)."

She just smiled and said, "Degas" with a funny kind of accent and handed me a book. Odd how teachers always give you books to look at when you ask them questions.

I forgot all about the girl until recess. I looked up at the tiny room and saw a little tiny room and nothing else. I thought maybe everyone was right. But, maybe... Nah.

I stood looking at the room the entire recess and Mr. Ellis came over and said, “Is everything all right Penelope?”

Mr. Ellis was the sixth grade teacher, and he was tall and handsome. He had soft features and thin brown hair. He wore glasses, but he always took them off to rub his nose. All the girls in the sixth grade had a crush on him.

I just said, “No I’m fine,” and walked towards Stephanie and her group of friends.

As I was walking towards the group I said, “How was your weekend Steph,…” but the bell rang, and I got cut off.

We had to line up and go in. Lining up to go in was somewhat of an adventure. Everyone was always talking and fooling until the teachers arrived to take us in. Most days Michael had to be told to stop fooling around and straighten out. He wasn't the only one, but he had to be told every day.

During Social Studies a little dust blew out from the big cage door in my classroom. Well, let me explain this. In the olden days they had heat, which came from a set of vents, which went through the entire school. They were all connected in the middle inside the walls, and that's how the rooms used to be heated. The vents were so large that we kids could fit right inside them. The vents looked like big animal cages inside the wall, and we could only see the front of it. They had crisscross bars on the front of them, because of these bars little holes were created. That's how the dust flew out into the classroom. The cages were all painted green. On the front of each cage there was a chain to pull the vent open and close. All of these vents were closed up now, and we had modern heaters in the classrooms.

It was too expensive to close these vents up entirely, so they were just there. It was a hole in the wall, a big hole with a screen attached on the front. Occasionally a little dust blew out of them, and we would clean it up. On this day there was a lot of dust coming out of the vent, but no one seemed to be concerned about it. Mrs. Neederman asked Cara and I to clean it up. Hmmmmm! I was very curious about the fact that dust was coming out of it today, and I stared at the vent for a very long time.

That night at supper Mom said, "How was your day Dear? Do you have much homework? I can help you later if you need me."

Before I could answer her, the phone rang, and my mom got up to answer it. I put my dish in the sink and went upstairs to do my homework. It wasn't my night to do the dishes. My mom and I switched nights clearing the dinner dishes. My mom always ended up helping me and letting me out of the heavy work like pans.

She always said, "Go do your homework. It's more important than dishes."

I couldn't figure out the math problems, so I picked up the phone to call Stephanie.

I heard my mom say into the phone, "Sure I can come to Chicago to help out, but what about Penelope?" "She has school?"

I recognized my Aunt Susan's voice right away, and she said, "Is there somebody she can stay with for a month or so?"

And that's when I put down the phone, a month or so? What could have happened?

I was sleeping when mom came into my room to say goodnight. Well, I was pretending to anyway.

She kissed me on the forehead and said, "Goodnight Penelope I love you."

As I was drifting off to real sleep I heard a whistle blowing far away, and I wondered why someone would be blowing a whistle so late at night and for what? This was the second time I heard a whistle blow late at night. I thought I knew every sound that my town made at night, and a whistle wasn't one of them.

On the way to school the next day Mom said, "I'm leaving for Chicago on Friday. I know this is sudden, but Aunt Susan really needs my help. How do you feel about this Penelope?"

Friday? That was two days away.

"Well, Mom," I said, as I was opening the car door, "I'll be fine. School isn't over yet, and if she really needs you then you must go."

Mom got out of the car and gave me a big kiss.

"You know Penelope you are so mature for your age. You are the best daughter anyone could ask for!"

To my dismay she embarrassed me, and I turned completely red right in front of the school. Good thing Ben or Michael weren't standing there. The teasing that would have ensued might have killed me.

She said Aunt Susan's husband had lost his job, and they have to relocate to another city. Mom was helping with the packing and the minding of the kids while Aunt Susan was at school. You see she was a teacher, and she couldn't leave for four weeks yet. But, they sold their house and had to leave at the same time school gets out. So Aunt Susan needed my mom's help.

Aunt Susan and my mom had been really close all their lives. They only had each other and no other siblings. They hadn't seen much of each other since Aunt Susan moved to Chicago with her husband and family. So, Aunt Susan moving to New York, which was much closer to us here in Massachusetts, was very exciting. We could visit much more often now.

I guessed I was staying with Mrs. Munson. Until a few weeks ago that would have been awful. Now that I knew Mrs. Munson, it didn't seem all that bad. I was kind of okay with it. I had never been away from my mom for more than a few days, and I knew it was going to be difficult. My mom was very determined to help her sister, so I guess I could sacrifice too.

As I drifted off to sleep I heard the whistle blow again. It was off in the distance and kind of soft. I tried to make a mental note to ask someone about it.

Chapter Eight
Mrs. Munson, Again!

Mrs. Munson let me walk to school. I thought I was in heaven. I mean it was only five blocks, but it was FUN!!! All the kids in the neighborhood that walked to school were surprised to see me. They got used to me very fast, and soon they were ringing Mrs. Munson's doorbell every morning looking for me. She would let them in and give them the special treat she had just baked for us. We all enjoyed the muffins, pancakes, and blueberry scones. I was putting on weight, but like I said, I needed it.

I forgot all about the pain in my belly from my mom being gone, the girl in the room and the whistle blowing at night. My mom called every night at nine to say goodnight. I told her all about Mrs. Munson, the kids and the treats. I was having so much fun. Everyday was just as fun as the next. Even Ben came over, and he brought a few of his buddies with him. I think they really enjoyed the blueberry scones the best. School was flying by!

At around ten-thirty one night I heard the whistle blow again. It was loud this time, and it blew three times. This was one too many times for me. I decided to go outside to listen and look. I know you probably think this is crazy, but Mrs. Munson slept very soundly, and I could be as quiet as a mouse.

I slipped on my jeans, a sweater, and my new white sneakers and went out the back door. The back door had a slight creak to it, but

I opened and shut it just right, so you couldn't really hear the creak.
It was a crisp night, and in certain places I could see my breath. I probably should have taken a jacket too. Sometimes May can be very cold in New England.

I started walking in the direction of the whistle. As I was walking down the sidewalk I thought it would be best for me to remain unseen by passing cars. I walked very closely to the edge of the sidewalk and tried to hide behind trees and bushes that grew along the way. Only two cars passed by, and I'm sure that they did not see me. As I was walking I realized that the sound led straight to the school? Hmmmm? Maybe it was a school whistle? I don't remember ever hearing a whistle at the school, especially this late at night. I wonder what it could be for?

Then I saw her running really fast towards the back of the school! Her hair was flying in the wind!

I ran as fast as I could after her. My legs felt as if they weighed a hundred pounds each. I couldn't even lift them. When I came around the back corner of the school... she was gone? It was the same girl from the lookout. I knew it! She did have long hair, and she was tall and thin and had on ripped blue jeans.

But where could she go so fast? I ran around the back of the school and started to check some things out. I couldn't really see anything. It was dark back there, and I got scared really quickly. I looked at the back door to the school, and I didn't notice anything strange about it. I looked at the windows that were close to the ground and they all looked fine. I walked around the recess yard and looked for some clues. NOTHING!

Perplexed I started walking back home hiding in the shadows so no one would see me. This time no cars passed by me, and I decided that it must be very late. I started to yawn, and then I knew it was late. I walked quickly. It was colder now and the wind started to pick up. It has snowed in May before, and I didn't have a jacket on.

When I got home I realized what I had done, and I felt ashamed. Mrs. Munson was so trusting. I would tell her tomorrow.

When I woke up and went downstairs for breakfast there were two police officers in the kitchen having coffee. I sat down to eat my breakfast. It was scrambled eggs, toast, home fries and a corn muffin. The kids came to the door at eight and came right in. Mrs. Munson gave them some corn muffins and told them to wait outside while I finished eating my breakfast. I was nervous eating, so I really didn't finish it at all.

I got up to leave for school, and one of the police officers said to me, " Good morning Penelope did you hear anything odd outside your bedroom window last night?"

I wondered how he knew my name?

I said. "No sir, I went to bed around nine-thirty and fell asleep very soon after that."

I could not tell the police officers that I had been out in the middle of the night. I hadn't even told Mrs. Munson yet. Now it looked like I never would!

Chapter Nine
The Girl

All day I was nervous in school. Even Mrs. Neederman commented on my behavior.

"Penelope you're as nervous as a cat today what's wrong?" she said this as she was erasing the board near my desk.

I just said, "Nothing" and smiled and continued doing my math problems.

The math problems were very difficult, and they required all of my attention.

At recess I stared up at the little room and wondered if she was up there. Was she watching me? Did she know who I was? Where did she go to school? Did she go to school?

So many questions, I had to find out! I just had to!

My lunch was extra special that day, but I couldn't eat a bite. I gave most of it away and threw the rest away. I felt really badly about throwing it away, but I just couldn't eat it. What was that girl up to anyway? Where was she going? Was she really in the school? I had to know. I just had to know!

Walking home Stephanie said, "Penelope can I come over after supper to do some homework? I think I understand the math problems, but if we do them together it would be easier."

I was too nervous, and I said," Mrs. Munson and I are going out for a little while, and I don't know what time we'll be back?"

I didn't like lying to my best friend, but I had to make some plans about this girl.

As we were eating dinner Mrs. Munson said," Do you want to go to the mall after we finish eating? I saw a cute pair of jeans there last week that would be perfect for you."

I didn't even hear her, and she had to ask me twice I guess.

"Nellie… Penelope are you feeling all right?" asked Mrs. Munson.

Mrs. Munson was really sweet and was trying to make my stay with her pleasant.

"Yes …Yes, I'm fine. I just have a bit of a headache. I think I'll go lie down." I mustered up.

I think Mrs. Munson was concerned because I heard her talking on the phone to one of her friends about me as I sat in my room and contemplated what to do.

That night I went to bed early around eight. When my mother called, I pretended I was asleep because she definitely would have known something was wrong by the sound of my voice. Mrs. Munson knocked, but I never answered. I heard her tell my mother I was looking tired, and she was glad I went to bed early. I felt so guilty, but I guess I was kind of tired from being out so late the night before. And... I planned on doing the same thing tonight! I had been doing so many things I had never done before, and I wondered if I would have done the same things if my mother were here?

At around ten-thirty that night I went down into the kitchen to get a glass of milk. What I was really doing was checking to see if Mrs. Munson was asleep; I was also looking for a flashlight. I checked the drawers in the kitchen carefully but no flashlight. Then I checked the hall closet. Ureeka! There was a flashlight on the top shelf in the closet. It figures it was on the top shelf where I couldn't reach it. I cautiously dragged a chair across the kitchen floor to the closet. I couldn't believe Mrs. Munson didn't wake up. It sounded like there was a herd of elephants in the kitchen! I got the flashlight and returned the chair.

I could hear her breathing heavy, and I figured I was safe. I skipped the milk and ran up to my room two stairs at a time. I threw on some clothes and grabbed a jacket. I didn't want to be cold again. The last thing I needed was to get sick. I snuck out the back door quietly. As I was shutting the back door it creaked really loudly. I stood frozen in horror and waited for Mrs. Munson to come out of her room. I stood there for what seemed like an hour. When she didn't come out of the room I breathed a heavy sigh of relief. Somehow I didn't think this was crazy, but I bet my mom and Mrs. Munson would.

I tried to hide in the shadows again while walking towards the school, so no one would see me. There wasn't anyone out driving this time, but you never know. When I got to the school I walked around to the back and sat on the hill. The ground was cold, hard, and had some dew on it. I sat on my jacket. There wasn't a breeze or anything, so I didn't need to put it on yet. I was trying to focus on the back door of the school thinking this would be where she would come out. It was dark, and I really couldn't see anything all that well. I didn't want to use the flashlight just yet, as it might scare the girl away. I was sitting under the trees and thinking about what to do next. I guess she didn't see me, but there she was right in front of me! The infamous running girl was sneaking out of the school by the back vent. This vent was part of the same system that was used to heat the school in the olden days. I couldn't really see how she got out, just that she was right there in front of me.

I was just about to say something to her, when I slipped on the grass and tumbled down the hill right onto the playground. The flashlight rolled across the recess yard and hit the basketball hoop leg. I cut my knee under my jeans, and I could feel the blood starting to run down my bare leg. I winced at the pain. She ran off towards the right side of the school without a word. When I managed to get up and run around the corner, she was gone, again!

This really upset me, so I sat for a while and thought about what I should do. Then it came to me; I would sneak in the vent the way she had snuck out. I walked towards the back of the school and found the vent and looked at it. I flashed the light on it, but I did not see a way to open it. I pushed it; I pulled it; and I kicked it! Nothing! How in the world did she get out? It was nailed up tightly. By this point blood was dripping on my new sneaker, and I figured it was time for me to go home. I kind of limped home, and my knee hurt like anything.

I limped up the back stairs and turned the doorknob. The back door was locked!! I couldn't believe it! I panicked and started to cry. My knee was really throbbing, and it felt like it was on fire, and now I couldn't get in. As I sat there crying, I heard Mrs. Munson's voice in my head. It sounded so real that it startled me. " I'll leave a key under this rock near this bush just in case I'm not here when you come home from school." She had always been there, so I never checked to see if it was really there. Now I was counting on it.

I tried to unlock the door quietly and sneak in. The door was very old, and it squeaked so! I thought for sure the whole neighborhood would wake up. It was eleven thirty by now, and I was exhausted. I couldn't wait to go to bed. I never thought I'd ever say that.

After I cleaned my knee and threw my clothes in the hamper, I took a quick shower. Boy, was I tired. I fell asleep almost instantly. Seven o'clock came really early, and when Mrs. Munson came to the door to call me for school I didn't even hear her call me at all.

"Penelope, Penelope, it's time to wake up!"

When I finally woke up it was nine-thirty. I was astonished by what had happened. I had slept late and missed school. I lazily padded downstairs and saw Mrs. Munson sorting laundry in the hall.

As she was sorting laundry she said to me, "Good morning sleepy head. How are you?"

I couldn't even answer her because she had my jeans in her hand. The KEY!!! I had forgotten about the key! What could I do? It was in my jeans pocket.

I stood for a while watching Mrs. Munson and thinking about

what I should do. I could grab the jeans and run? She was just about to empty my clothes hamper when the doorbell rang. Saved by the bell! I rushed over to the hamper and reached into my jeans pocket. Whew! But, NO KEY!!? I reached into the other pocket, NO KEY!!!? Where is it? What could I have done with it? I started to cry. Just then Mrs. Munson came into the room.

"What ever is the matter with you Nellie? You look rather flushed, you must be coming down with something."

She put her hand to my forehead.

"You don't look good. This morning when I went into your room you wouldn't budge, and now your forehead is so warm. You get yourself right up to bed and lie down. I'll bring you up some tea and toast."

I didn't know what to say. By the time she came up to my room I was fast asleep.

When I woke up it was dark out. Wow, could I have slept for that long? I had never done that before. Then again I had never snuck out of my house in the middle of the night either.

Just then the phone rang.

Mrs. Munson called up to me, "Telephone Penelope."

Expecting my mother I put on my sick voice. I was sure Mrs. Munson would tell her about today and being sick and all, so I didn't want to act like I was well.

"HH EE ll OOO," I said slowly into the receiver.

"Where were you today?" screeched Stephanie's voice into the phone?

"Oh Stephanie I felt sick today, so I stayed home." I said.

"You'll never believe what happened in school today?" She rambled on, "They found an old red sneaker under the principal's desk, an old red sneaker? And a key! A key? Now whose is that? No one claimed either thing they found, and she locks her office door every night. How did they get there?"

She was rather excited, but not being there myself, I couldn't muster up much energy in my voice.

"That's unbelievable Stephanie." I mumbled into the phone.

"It's a mystery, a real mystery! Please come to school tomorrow so we can help solve it!" she finally said, as we were ending our conversation.

As I hung up the phone I realized that the sneaker must belong to the running girl? And the key must be mine? Did she have another pair of sneakers? Did she really have my key? What was she going to do with it if she did? What should I do? I guess I must have been really sick because I fell right back to sleep.

Chapter Ten
The Police

While Ben and I were walking to school, I noticed a few police cars go by. I didn't think anything of it.

"Ben, what do you think all those police cars are for?" I asked him softly.

"How should I know Nellie I'm thinking about my math homework, I didn't do it."

Neither of us could figure it out, but I was the nervous one. When we got to school we saw two police cars and a crowd of people where we usually line up to go into school.

Quickly we ran over to the crowd. In the crowd I saw the four teenagers that Ben and I had seen the week before. I thought maybe they had something to do with the red sneaker and the key. It turns out that they skipped school and were throwing rocks up at the lookout early this morning and someone had called the police. Jeezzee , nothing too exciting.

The principal clapped her hands when the bell rang, and we all lined up. Mrs. Villanus was not a very pretty principal, and she had a weird twitch. She was short and kind of fat, well I don't think it's nice to say that, but it's true. Her hair was frizzy and she didn't take care of it. But, she was in charge of the entire school, and we all got used to her somehow. The previous principal Mr. Mularkey was just so pleasant that no one could ever take his place. He's retired now and he lives in Florida or South Africa. I'm not sure.

In school that day I kept hearing weird noises coming from the big vents in the room. They weren't very loud noises; it sounded like someone moving things across the floor. One time I even thought I heard someone whisper my name. By this point I thought I was losing my mind. No one else but me had heard this. I even thought someone was watching me or us. I could feel the eyes on me. I didn't see anything, but I felt it.

Stephanie and Emma waited for me to go to lunch. We sat at the very last table, so we could talk privately about the red sneaker, the key and the weirdness I felt. The assistant principal was on duty for lunch today. Everyone liked Ms. Eavn even if her name was pronounced EVEN. She was older than Mrs. Neederman but younger than Mrs. Villanus. She had short blonde hair with bangs and always wore a sweater. She had us eat up quickly, so we could go out into the "cool spring afternoon."

Stephanie, Emma, and I discussed the red sneaker, the key and the weirdness. Emma was my friend too, but she lived kind of far from school, so I didn't see her very often outside of school. She was short and had very short brown hair with bangs. She always had a clip in it to keep the bangs out of her eyes. We made a plan to come to the school that very night to investigate the doors and windows. I could tell they were afraid to go out at night, but I convinced them everything would be fine.

Emma would sleep over Stephanie's house and, "It would only take about an hour" I said.

I did not tell them that I had been there two times before. Some things are personal.

The police interviewed a few of the teachers, and we had to do some work at our seats. It was boring, and we didn't have any homework because we did all of our work in school. All day I felt sick to my stomach. Maybe I was really sick. That would stink especially with all the plans we had just made.

Devon Holmes sits next to me in class.

After lunch he said to me, "Penelope did you understand the math last night?"

I just nodded my head as Mrs. Neederman was beginning Math class.

"Boys and girls would you please take out your homework so we can correct it."

Everyone took out the homework except Michael.

As Mrs. Neederman was walking towards Michael she said, "Michael do you have your assignment from last night?"

Michael's head was down very low.

"No Mrs. Neederman I lost it."

"You lost your homework Michael?" Mrs. Nederman replied.

"Yes, I did" Michael said sheepishly.

Mrs. Neederman didn't seem very happy and said. "Well, Michael you realize that this is the third time you haven't done your homework in a month. Correct?"

"Yes, Mrs. Neederman" was all Michael could get out.

As Mrs. Neederman was walking towards her desk she said, "Please see me at recess, so we can discuss this further."

I thought Michael was going to fall off his chair. That's the worst when a teacher says please come see me at recess. You know you're in trouble!

When we left for the day Mrs. Neederman gave us all a piece of candy, and told us to be careful on the way home. She gave us candy at least once a week, and we thought it was the greatest! She was probably the best teacher I had ever had, but the kids are the only ones who ever really know that.

Walking home Ben and Josh from grade four were playing catch with a football, and it hit Mary Agnes from grade three right in the head. She started crying, and her big sister Martha started yelling at Ben and Josh, and it got really confusing and noisy.

"Martha it was an accident" I said as I came closer to her.

"Mind your own business Nellie" she said as she started chasing Ben.

" I didn't mean to hit her in the head" Ben said as he was running past Martha.

I ran all the way home. I didn't want to be involved in anything else.

When I got home the police were at Mrs. Munson's house again.

This time they said, “Did you see a young girl running around the neighborhood last night Miss?”

They showed me a picture of the girl I had seen up in the lookout. Well, I couldn’t very well tell them I had seen her last night because that would mean that I also would have been out at night. I didn’t want Mrs. Munson to get upset with my mother and me...oh goodness!

So I just said, “I may have seen her out my window, but I’m not positive, and I don’t know for sure.” Fortunately they accepted my answer and went to Ben’s house.

Later I said to Mrs. Munson, ”Why are the police looking for her?” “What’s the big deal?”

As she was clearing the table she said, “ I think they are concerned for her safety. There have been some strange things going on in town, and they’re interviewing everyone that lives close to North Side Elementary School.”

Concerned for **her** safety?
What did that mean?

Chapter Eleven
The Vents

Stephanie, Emma and I met at ten-thirty outside Mrs. Munson's back door. I never did tell them that the key might be mine. I just left a piece of paper stuck in the door, so I could get back in. Stephanie brought a whistle and Emma had a flashlight.

Emma said as we were walking toward the school, "I had to put new batteries in this, I hope it works."

I had string just in case we got lost inside the school.

As we approached the back of the school we noticed some clothes lying in a heap on the ground in front of the grate where the girl came out the last time I saw her there. The clothes didn't look new but they weren't dirty either. I didn't touch the clothes and decided to put our plan into action. Stephanie blew the whistle, and we all held our breath. Nothing happened. We waited a few more minutes, and then I asked Stephanie to blow the whistle again. Our patience paid off. The grate slid sideways and invited us in. I figured the whistle was how the girl got in and got out so quickly. She blew the whistle, and her brothers inside pulled a chain and the grate slid open. Genius!

Now I knew why I couldn't get in before. The grate didn't push in or pull out. It slid sideways! It was very dark and damp through the grate, and if we didn't
have the flashlight we couldn't have seen a thing.

Emma switched on the flashlight and said. "Whew I'm glad this works," and it illuminated the entire room.

WOW! It was dirty and smelly in there, and there was a path clearly made that led upwards. We all looked at each other and without saying a word continued to walk up what seemed to be a path that led to??? It was a door with an exit sign over it. Only the E was lit up, and it was hanging on its side. Dust and years of neglect was the only thing you could see. The door was locked.

Emma turned the knob and said, "Ick, it's all dirty." She wiped her hand on her jeans.

There were so many spider webs with flies in them and spiders that I held my breath and closed my eyes every time I passed one. I swear I even saw a mouse or two. I couldn't.... no I wouldn't... scream. It would definitely give us away.

We could hear loud clanking noises, and we jumped every time we heard them. The whirring noises were impossible to talk through, so we just kept walking silently until we came to a fork. We supposed that the noises were the heat. Now I'm not as brave as you may think I am, but I was the one that suggested we spilt up at this point and use the string so we could go explore, and then meet back here and report.

I think I let out a huge sigh of relief when the girls said, "NO WAY! We stick together," but the whirring noises must have drowned out my big sigh.

It was cold and dark, and we were going nowhere. I was about to suggest that we turn back when we came into a room. It was a warm and dimly lit room. It had books and clothes and shoes on every bit of furniture in the room. We were so startled that Emma dropped the flashlight, and it rolled under the table noisily. There was a couch made of leather, two chairs that dads usually sit in all comfy with footstools, a kitchen table with four chairs all painted black and a TV stand with a TV on it that looked as if it worked.

There was a small refrigerator in the corner and a hot plate. I didn't know what that was used for, but Stephanie did.

She said, "We use one when we go camping. It heats up the food really well. You need a plug for it, and sometimes we have to use a real fire to heat stuff up. When that happens my mom gets really upset."

On top of the refrigerator there was a loaf of bread and a bag of potato chips.

There were wrappers from food scattered about. The wrappers looked familiar to me, and I realized that they were the same wrappers as the food from the cafeteria at school. It was not very good food, so I never got it, although the pizza it seems was quite tasty according to Duane.

This room had all the comforts of home, except no one was here. There were three beds in the adjoining room all neatly made up with old bed covers, but clean ones. They each had a pillow on them and a blanket at the foot of the bed. The blankets were all different, and one had a hole in it. There was a small lamp on a table beside the very first bed. The lamp was old, and it had a cloth over it to mute the light coming out of it. The sink had dishes in it but only a few. It appeared to us that someone had left in a hurry.

In the center of the room was a winding staircase. It was black and metal and had a lot of rusty spots on it. There were books piled on some of the stairs but not too many. It didn't really look safe, but we had come this far. I was the first to start up the stairs. Emma didn't think we should go up, and Stephanie was right behind me.

As we were climbing the stairs Stephanie said, “Boy, I hope this is worth it Nellie my mom would kill me if she knew I was here.”

I said hastily as we started to climb, “Yeah I know, mine would too.”

In the end we all climbed those stairs not knowing what we were going to find.

When we got up to the top we were amazed at what we found! On the floor was a complete map of the stars. Beautifully drawn. It looked like someone drew them then made the constellations around the star groupings. It was a work of art. As we looked out the window we could see the houses all lit up by the moon. There was a telescope dismantled in the corner, and books and pencils and drawings all over the floor. This was the little room that had captured my imagination for so long. It was an observatory, how beautiful!

We could not for the life of us figure out what these rooms were all about. We sat down and started to discuss what the main room might be for.

Emma said, "Maybe the room is for the custodian Mr. Murphy?"

We all knew that Mr. Murphy lived on Laurel Hill Lane in a big white house with red shutters. He had two dogs and a parakeet. One dog was a German Shepard, and the other one was a Poodle. He brought the parakeet to school once or twice a year for show and tell. There were no water bowls for the dogs, and we did not see a cage for the parakeet. We decided Mr. Murphy was out.

Then Olivia said, "Maybe the room is for the principal. Do you think maybe she comes here to rest?"

We soon dismissed that idea because I couldn't picture her in the room with the ripped blankets.

We were getting tired of all this supposing this and supposing that, when we heard a scary noise. Not a loud one like the whirring or the clanking of the pipes, but a soft noise like someone going by. We all stared at each other and ran to the middle of the room and screamed and hugged. It was kind of weird, but I felt much better. Soon after that, a boy appeared, then another boy appeared, and then a girl. It was her!!!

Chapter Twelve
The Robinson's

Mrs. Munson came to pick me up after school the next day. I couldn't figure out why she was here. Every other day she had let me walk home with my friends. Why not today?

As we were driving home she said,
"The police came by again, and they are telling everyone to be watchful of everything. I feel safer picking you up. How about we go for an ice cream cone BEFORE dinner?"

As we were eating our cones she said, "I guess someone has been rummaging through the Goodwill bins at the town hall, and there was a hotplate missing from the town library break room. It's quite a mystery around town, and the police are trying to solve it."

I just licked my cone quietly.

I knew where those things were. I felt guilty for not telling Mrs. Munson the first thing that morning. I was just going to tell Mrs. Munson all about the night before, and about my wanderings when my mother's blue Volvo came pulling into my driveway as Mrs. Munson's gray Buick pulled into her driveway. I jumped out of the gray Buick so fast; I swear it was still moving. I was so happy to see my mom that I forgot all about the girl and the boys and the clothes and the hotplate and everything.

We went out to dinner that night, and she told me all about Aunt Susan, her husband, her family, and just about everything that happened in Chicago. I told her about Mrs. Munson, the fun, and the healthy food.

I left out the part about the soda, the junk food, and the ice cream BEFORE dinner. I thought the part about walking to school everyday was better left unsaid too.

I left all of that for Mrs. Munson to tell. Mrs. Munson had a way about her that made my mother feel safe. My stomach felt warm inside the way it did before my mom went to Chicago. I left out the sneaking out part too.

I guess my mom had met a Mrs. Robinson on the plane home from Chicago. She started telling me about her when the phone rang.

It was Stephanie and she yelled into the phone, "Get over here right away!"

I told my mother I'd be right back and ran to Stephanie's house. She had been out sick from school that day, and I was dying to talk to her.

Stephanie said, as I was coming in the door, "What do you think about those three children we met?" I can't seem to put it together?"

I guess my mouth just about opened to the floor, and then it hit me!

My mother had met a woman on the plane, and before I left, my mom said, "that this Mrs. Robinson had three children."

Three children, oh my, I get it??

"The girl and the two boys are called the Robinsons," I yelled to Stephanie. "They are her children. They must live in the school!"

Stephanie just stared at me with a confused expression on her face.

You see when the children came into the room that night we snuck into the school. We all just screamed and scared them away. Then the three of us ran home in the dark. We ran so fast that we forgot to ask them anything.

I left Stephanie's house and ran all the way home to get the rest of the story from my mom. She told me the story after I calmed down.

Their father had been a local artist, and he had died in an accident at the mill a few years earlier. The mother stayed in town and lived in the house as long as she could until the bank took it away from her. You see she couldn't pay the bills, and the bank took their house away.

Mrs. Robinson was very upset and decided to go back to Chicago where she was originally from and try to find a job and a place to live. The children were to stay here with Mrs. Robinson's sister their aunt, Mrs. Hilder. Mrs. Hilder agreed to take the children, but when Mrs. Robinson never showed up with the children she went to visit her other sister in Yarmouth, Ma. Mrs. Robinson left and assumed the children were with Mrs. Hilder, and that's where the confusion begins.

Chapter Thirteen
Finally

Secrets are never good to keep from people, especially the ones you care about most. Now all that sneaking around that I did was really harmless, but if I had told someone earlier the Robinson kids would have been safe a lot sooner.

You see Darlene, Thomas, and Andrew, (the Robinson's), were living in the school's heating system and going to school everyday while we were. They were listening at the grates to all the lessons. They really missed going to school and wanted to hear what was going on. Thomas was in fourth grade and so was

Andrew. They were twins. They were not identical twins but fraternal twins. That means they didn't look exactly alike. I think that's a good thing. I wouldn't want to be called the wrong name all the time like the identical twins in the sixth grade, Mary and Marianne.

Thomas was short even for a fourth grader and Andrew was kind of tall. They both had brown hair and very blue eyes. Andrew wore glasses, and his hair was longer than his brothers. Darlene was tall and thin. She had medium length hair, but it was a very light color brown. Her clothes looked as if they didn't fit her, but she was clean.

They couldn't go to their old school because everyone there knew that their mother was in Chicago. The reason the dust came out in my class was because Darlene is in fifth grade, so she listened at the grate in my class. She's tall for her age and skinny, but she sure is smart.

Imagine living in a school's ventilation system for two months while your mother is in Chicago!

Darlene went rummaging through the Goodwill boxes for clothes for her brothers and herself to wear. She took the hotplate from the library. Well you have to eat. Darlene planned to return it to the library when she was finished with it. It wasn't easy living like this, but she had to do it for her mom. Darlene couldn't call her mother because she didn't actually know her exact location, and her belly ached too. So, I guess my finding her has made us BFF's.

Darlene's mother was questioned by the police. But, she was so busy in Chicago and had very little money that the time just flew by, and before she knew it she was on her way back to see her children. Her sister was probably the most trusted person that Mrs.

Robinson knew, so she never suspected a thing.

It was all a big mix up, and I'm glad I solved it with the help of my two friends, Stephanie and Emma. I'm still not sure where my key is and I wonder if the one in the principal's office is mine? I guess I'll have to come up with a way to find that out. Now what about that red sneaker in the principals' office?????

ABOUT THE AUTHOR

C.C.Beechum lives in Massachusetts with her two sons Thomas and Andrew. She enjoys reading, cleaning (seriously), and having fun. She has recently started golfing and can hit the ball straight, but not very far. She has recently had two poems published in the book *Sauced.*

Email the author at:
ccbeechum@yahoo.com

50395215R00077

Made in the USA
Lexington, KY
14 March 2016